MY TEACHER LOOKS LIKE ME

AUTUMN DODSON

This book belongs to

....

....

The book is dedicated to my Aunt Edna. At the beginning of 2021, Aunt Edna was 95 years old when she passed away due to COVID-19. When Aunt Edna was in elementary school, she attended Nelson Merry, which was segregated at the time. Just weeks before Aunt Edna passed away, she facetimed the students in my class to give a first-hand account on what it was like to go to school before the Civil Rights Movement. Aunt Edna always valued education and supported my dreams of becoming a teacher.

Aunt Edna was an amazing person! I just want her to know that I love and miss her very much!

My name is Naomi, which means joy. I am an eight-year-old girl who lives in Peachtree Corners, Georgia.

Summertime is the best time for every kid, except when they realize that school is starting in a few days! It was the end of the summer, and I was **DREADING** going back to school.

I know what you are thinking. No kid likes going to school, but my reasons for dreading school are different than most. You probably will not understand, but I will try to explain anyway.

Reason #1

No one **EVER** says my name right. My mom always tells me that she knew I would bring so much joy in her life, which is why she decided to name me Naomi. However, I do not think she ever considered the lack of joy I would feel when I have to constantly correct the way people pronounce my name. Even my teachers, who are supposed to be the smartest people in the world, say my name incorrectly.

Alice   Bella   Addie   Harper

Alice, Bella, Addie, and Harper are some of my really good friends. Although they are really nice, they do not understand why I am constantly complaining about people pronouncing my name wrong. This is probably because everyone always says their names right.

I cannot help but wonder how nice it would be to have a normal name that people say correctly the first time. I bet the girls with these names never have to worry about people pronouncing their names wrong.

Reason #2

It takes my mom **FOREVER** to do my hair! There are even times when I miss the school bus because my hair just does not cooperate. My hair is very curly and coiled, but I just wish it could be straight like all the other girls' hair in my class. My mom always tells me that my hair is beautiful. However, I do not think she realizes how embarrassing it is to be the last one to walk into class.

Reason #3

No one looks like me! All of my teachers look the same, all of my friends look the same, and you will not believe it, but even the walls of the school look the same. The school janitor, Ms. Cynthia, is the only one other person who looks like me. She reminds me of my Aunt Edna because she always has the warmest smile on her face. However, I only get to see her when she is cleaning the classroom at the end of the day.

I cannot help but wonder what it would be like if more people at school looked like the people in my family and the people at my church. I have been going to church my whole life, so the people at my church are basically like my family. I just wish I could find people outside of my family and the school janitor who look like me. This may not seem like a big deal to you, but this is my main reason for not wanting to go back to school.

Even though I have all these reasons that I dread going to school, my mom tells me that I have to go anyway.

The night before the first day of school has finally come. I am talking with my friend Julia about going back to school.

I try to tell her the different reasons I am dreading going back, but she just does not understand why I am making such a big deal about it.

Julia says that it should not matter that people do not say my name correctly because some names are just hard to pronounce. She also says that I should like my hair because people always want to touch it since it looks so cool. As I tell Julia about my last and most important reason, she laughs and says, " Naomi, the only bad part of not having someone who looks like you at school is that it will be hard to find a partner for twin day."

She probably does not see why it is a big deal to me because people always say her name right the first time, her hair is nice and straight, and all the people at school look like her.

Finally, I hang up the phone and walk downstairs. My mom decides to do my hair because she does not want me to be late for the first day of school tomorrow. Then, she kisses me good night, and says, "Naomi, I think you are going to have a great school year. Get some rest."

Before I go to sleep, I kneel next to my bed and say my nightly prayers. In my prayers, I ask God very nicely to send someone who looks like me, even if it is just only one person. As I was laying in bed, I thought about what Julia said. Maybe the reasons I dread going back to school are not that big of a deal.

In the morning, the smell of strawberry muffins and bacon wake me up. When it is a special day, my mom always makes my favorite breakfast.

I brush my teeth and get ready for school. I am so happy that my mom did my hair last night. It gave me an extra 30 minutes to watch my favorite cartoons before we had to leave. "Naomi, let's go!" said my mom.

As she drops me off, she kisses me on my forehead and says, "Remember your room number is 136! Also, don't forget your name means joy, so be sure you bring joy into someone's life today." I wave goodbye to my mom, and I instantly start to think about my three reasons again.

As I walk into school, everything was exactly how I remember. The teachers look the same, my friends look the same, and you will not believe it, but even the walls of the school still look the same. As I got closer to my classroom, I had a feeling that something about this year was going to be different.

I start to walk down the second-grade hallway, and I see a woman who I had never seen before. She is smiling and waving. I realize that the woman who is smiling and waving is also standing outside of Room 136. I quickly remember, THAT'S MY CLASS!

As I approach the door, a woman with curly black hair is smiling and waving at me. "Hi, Naomi! I am Ms. Young. I will be your second-grade teacher, and I am SO excited to have you in my class this year. Come in and find your desk!"

I could not believe it! For the first time in my life, my teacher pronounced my name correctly, without me even telling her how to say it. Ms. Young also had curly black hair just like mine. Most importantly, this is the first time that I saw someone at school besides the school janitor who looked like me.

When the bell rings, Ms. Young greets the class and says, "Hello, everyone! I am so excited to be your teacher this year. We are going to have a great year!" Ms. Young begins to tell the class all about herself. As the teacher is talking, I cannot help but to admire her.

She has curly and coiled hair just like mine! Her skin was caramel and brown just like mine! She shows the class a picture of her family, and you will not believe it, but they look just like my family and the people at my church!

Throughout the day, I make sure I do my best in everything Ms. Young asks the class to do. From getting out a pencil to lining up for lunch, I make sure I am the first to do it. I just want Ms. Young to be as impressed with me as I am with her.

As the day comes to an end, I am dreading going home. I am having such a good time at school with my teacher that I do not want to leave. The bell finally rings, and it is time to pack up for dismissal.

As I am leaving the classroom, Ms. Young pulls me to the side and says, "Naomi, I love how hard you were working in class today. I am so impressed by how well you follow directions. I also noticed that you are such a great leader. I am so glad that you are in my class. We are going to have a fantastic year. I hope you have a great afternoon. See you tomorrow!" I am so excited that I wanted to scream, but instead, I just give her a big smile and walk to dismissal.

When my car rider number is called, I rush to the car. Before my mom could even speak, I exclaim, "Mom! Mom! You will not believe it! I had the best day ever. Ms. Young pronounced my name right the FIRST TIME. Her hair was curly and coiled just like mine! She even has caramel and brown skin just like mine! Mom, pinch me. I think I am dreaming!"

My mom gives me a soft smile and says, "Naomi, this is great! I am glad that you no longer dread going to school".

As I was thinking to myself, the reasons I mentioned earlier went away once I saw Ms. Young standing outside my classroom door. In that moment, I could tell that this was going to be a great school year! I cannot wait for school tomorrow.

I look over at my mom and say, "I now see why you named me after joy. I have never felt more joy in my life than today when I finally met my teacher who looks like me!"

Be somebody who makes everybody feel like a somebody!!

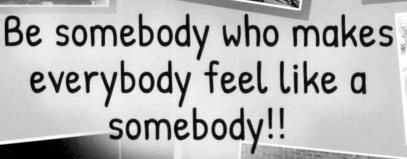